On My Way to the Bath

Sarah Maizes

illustrated by
Michael Paraskevas

Walker & Company
New York

First published in the United States of America in May 2012
by Walker Publishing Company, Inc., a division of Bloomsbury Publishing, Inc.
www.bloomsburykids.com

For information about permission to reproduce selections from this book, write to
Permissions, Walker BFYR, 175 Fifth Avenue, New York, New York 10010

Library of Congress Cataloging-in-Publication Data
Maizes, Sarah.
On my way to the bath / by Sarah Maizes ; illustrations by Michael Paraskevas.
      p.   cm.
Summary: Livi imagines herself as a snake, a gymnast, a rock star,
and more as she tries to avoid taking a bath.
ISBN 978-0-8027-2364-2 (hardcover) · ISBN 978-0-8027-2365-9 (reinforced)
[1. Baths—Fiction. 2. Imagination—Fiction.] I. Paraskevas, Michael, ill. II. Title.
PZ7.M27954On 2012   [E]—dc23   2011021942

Art created digitally with a Wacom Cintiq tablet in Painter and Photoshop
Typeset in Boopee and Latino Rumba
Book design by Donna Mark

Printed in China by C&C Offset Printing Co., Ltd., Shenzhen, Guangdong
2 4 6 8 10 9 7 5 3 1 (hardcover)
2 4 6 8 10 9 7 5 3 1 (reinforced)

For Izzy, Ben, and of course, Livi
—S. M.

As always, for my wonderful mother, Betty
—M. P.

I do not want to take a bath. Baths are boring.
Everything is more fun than baths.

On my way to the bath, I slither off the sofa. I am a snake. I slink, I slide. I stick my tongue out at my brother.

On my way to the bath, I see my blocks on the TV room floor. I will make a statue. It will be a statue of me. Holding a cat.

On my way to the bath, I do a cartwheel. I am a professional gymnastics girl. I bend, I balance and stretch... Watch me do a perfect split...

On my way to the bath, I see my sister in her room—she's listening to music. Hey, **I** can sing that song! **JUST** like a rock star...
"LA, LA, LA, LAAAAAAAA!!!!!!"
I will put on a show!

On my way to the bath, I pass the guinea pigs, Leo and Melly, my loyal minions. It's time to plan our latest caper. They will help me rule the world!

On my way to the bath, I march. I am in a marching band! I play tuba. As I march down the street, the crowd goes wild for my tuba solo! BWWWWWAAAAAHHHHHHH!

On my way to the bath, I pass through a jungle. A thick, dark jungle. I am looking for sloths. Oh no! Quicksand! I swing to safety!

On my way to the bath, I hide behind the bathroom door. I am a jungle cat . . . I see an unsuspecting gopher . . .

I get in.

I play. I use soap. I use my sea-horse washcloth to get very, very clean. Even my toes are clean. Toes are Sea Horse's specialty.

I am a shark . . .